THE VISION

By Jack Miller
Illustrated by Arkie Ring

all men are created equal

A POST HILL PRESS BOOK
ISBN: 978-1-63758-665-5

Post Hill Press
New York • Nashville
posthillpress.com

Published in the United States of America
1 2 3 4 5 6 7 8 9 10

This book belongs to

_____

Grandson says, "Pa, these are some of our friends from school, and we have been telling them some of the stories you were telling about when you were our age. They wanted to hear them, too."

Grandpa replies, "Well, David, when I was your age, the world was at war. There was no television in those days, but when we went to the movies on Saturday afternoons, we would see newsreels of our soldiers fighting the Germans in Europe and also the Japanese in the Pacific area."

"Because of the war, there were shortages of many things. For example, we could buy only a certain amount of meat and only a few gallons of gasoline a week because they were so needed for the war effort. We saved tin foil from gum and other packages and wrapped them into big balls to turn in for the war effort. We also saved and donated old tires and tin cans."

"As I remember, there was an American flag in every classroom, and every morning at our first class, we would stand up straight and proud and put our hand over our hearts and say the Pledge of Allegiance. 'I pledge allegiance to the Flag of the United States of America, and to the Republic for which it stands, one Nation under God, indivisible, with liberty and justice for all.'"

"Of course, we didn't know exactly what all of those words meant except that it made us proud to be Americans and it sort of made us feel as if we were supporting our soldiers somehow."

Olivia, the granddaughter, says, "We don't have flags in our classrooms and we say the Pledge of Allegiance only once a week on Fridays at assembly. But what do those words mean?"

Grandpa answers, "Well, as I think about it now, I realize that we weren't pledging allegiance just to our country, but to the ideals that our country stands for. We are really pledging allegiance to those ideals in our Declaration of Independence that 'All men are created equal,' and because they are all equal, they are all entitled to their 'Life, Liberty and the pursuit of Happiness' and more."

"It is those ideals, that vision for our country, that unites us—people from different countries, people of different skin colors, religions, nationalities, boys and girls, men and women, all of us united as Americans. As our Declaration says, we are all created equal. We all have the same human rights."

"It is that vision that not only unites us, but, as our pledge says, also makes us 'indivisible,' meaning that we all stand together as one on the road toward keeping and achieving even more of that vision."

Grandpa continues, "We have already come a long way on that journey, but, boys and girls, it is going to be your job to move us even closer toward that goal."

Tony says, "That's silly. We aren't all equal. Look at David, he's bigger and stronger than me, and Olivia is much smarter. She's the smartest one in the class. And Ella is the prettiest one in the class. How can you say we are all created equal?"

The grandfather reaches for a book and says, "Well, why don't we ask Mr. Jefferson what he meant? He's the one who wrote those words."

Thomas Jefferson magically appears.

Grandpa says, "Mr. Jefferson, these young people would like to know what you meant when you wrote that 'all men are created equal.' They look around and see that not everyone is equal. Some are stronger or prettier or smarter or a different color. I am sure you can explain what you meant."

Jefferson says, "Well, sir, of course there are outward differences in people. But in America, for the first time in the history of the world, we created a nation founded on the belief that everyone has the same basic rights. We call them natural rights because we have those rights from nature, not from the government. It is the role of the government to protect those rights, not to decide who gets them."

"Amongst those rights, for example, is the right to our lives, the right to our liberty, and the right to pursue our happiness, to make the most of our abilities."

"So, since we are born equal, that means that no one is born to rule over others. In other words, as I once wrote, some people are not born with a saddle on their backs while a favored few are born with boots and spurs ready to ride them."

"We are meant to be a self-ruling nation, a nation where the people are the ones who ultimately have the final say. But, for that to work, boys and girls, you must learn how to do that, how to preserve the liberty that our form of government is meant to protect."

Sam says, "How could you say that Mr. Jefferson? My ancestors were born as slaves. What rights did they have?"

Jefferson answers, "Young man, you are right. When I wrote those words, we had slavery in some of our states and even I owned slaves. I knew that it was a terrible wrong. And a few years later, when we wrote the Constitution, many states wanted to free the slaves, but other states refused to join the union if we did. So, we compromised with them just as you sometimes compromise when you can't win an argument."

"From what I can see, the country has come a long way toward achieving those rights for all. There is no more slavery, although it took a bloody civil war to end it. Many people, both black and white, died in that effort to make good on that promise of liberty for all, not just for some.

And even then, it wasn't a complete victory because discrimination, violence, and mistreatment continued. And since then, the country has been struggling and making progress in lots of ways to realize that vision that all men—which also means all women and everyone—are 'created equal' and have equal rights."

Jefferson continues, "This was the first time in the history of the world that a nation was founded on a principle. It is that principle, that vision that all men are created equal, that has encouraged so many people from all around the world to come to America to improve their lives through their own hard work."

"It is that freedom, to work hard (or not) and to enjoy the benefits of your efforts that made America so exceptional."

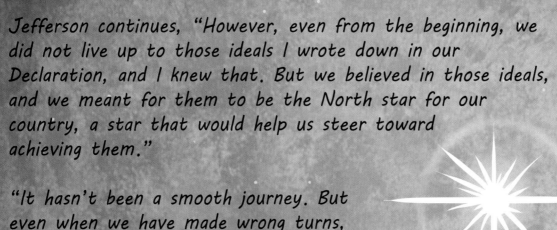

Jefferson continues, "However, even from the beginning, we did not live up to those ideals I wrote down in our Declaration, and I knew that. But we believed in those ideals, and we meant for them to be the North star for our country, a star that would help us steer toward achieving them."

"It hasn't been a smooth journey. But even when we have made wrong turns, that North Star, that vision, has helped us get back on course. So, if we continue to understand it and believe in it, we can continue to make progress toward achieving that vision."

vision

NOW

1776

Jefferson continues,
"Through the years, our country
has made great progress toward achieving that
ideal. And our country is getting closer. But, as
one of our presidents, Ronald Reagan, said, 'We
are only one generation away from losing our
freedom.'"

"And, if you don't want to be the generation
that loses it, you must become well informed
citizens to do your part in guiding us toward
even greater progress in achieving that goal. The
way toward achieving that progress is by building
on what others have done, not by tearing
it down."

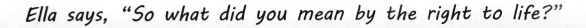

Ella says, "So what did you mean by the right to life?"

Jefferson answers, "Well, it is right there in the Ten Commandments where it says, 'Thou shalt not murder.' It means that so long as you respect the right to life for everyone else, no one is entitled to take your life. You have a right to your life."

Sam asks, "Mr. Jefferson, if liberty is a natural right, why is it okay to put some people in jail?"

Jefferson answers, "Well, Sam, our founders gave us a constitution that sets the ground rules for how we should act and for our protection against too strong of a government that may take away some of our rights. But the important part is that we are a nation of laws and we are all protected for equal treatment under the law. And when someone breaks a law and is convicted, then they often go to jail."

"But any laws that are made must be laws that are permitted by our Constitution. The Constitution was designed to protect the people so laws can't be made that take away any of the people's freedoms. If such a law is made, then it can be challenged in court and be struck down."

Olivia says, "Mr. Jefferson, you said we had a lot of rights, and you mentioned that we had the right to life and liberty, but you didn't say we have a right to happiness. You just said we have a right to 'the pursuit of happiness.' Why aren't we guaranteed happiness?"

Jefferson says, "Well, Olivia, that's a good question. You remember that when I said that along with the 'liberty' that is guaranteed comes responsibility."

"And, besides, life and liberty are the same for all. Happiness can be different for different people. Some people want to build empires and devote their time and effort to that...

...while others are happy making a decent living and having a lot of time to do other things. The only thing I have observed to be true for all is that people are happiest when they are self-sufficient, not dependent on others for their needs in life."

"The vision in our Declaration is that everyone should have an equal position at the starting line and then fair play along the way. But the rest is up to the individual and how well he or she does depends on their own ability and their own hard work. People with less ability often do better than others with more ability just because they work so much harder."

Olivia says, "But Mr. Jefferson, in your time, and even today, as you look around you, there are some people who are much richer than others, and there are many who barely make enough to live on. How is that equal? How is that fair?"

Jefferson answers, "Well, Olivia, in the first place, while all are born with equal rights, they are not all born with equal abilities or under equal conditions. But everyone has the ability to work hard and to make the most out of themselves. Each person is free to choose what they want to do to use their abilities to the best to achieve the most they can. Of course, we also have the responsibility to help take care of those who truly are incapable of taking care of themselves."

Grandpa says, "Thank you, Mr. Jefferson, for explaining what you meant when you wrote those words, that vision, in our Declaration of Independence."

"And, kids, your happiness is going to depend on your own actions. You are the ones who are responsible for your own actions, and your success and happiness in life will depend on the actions you choose."

"And now that you know what the words in our Declaration—as well as the words in our Pledge of Allegiance—mean, I would like all of you to join me in saying that pledge."